POPPY

the Pirate Dog's
New Shipmate

D1378312

POPPY
the Pirate Dog's
New Shipmate

Liz Kessler
illustrated by Mike Phillips

CANDLEWICK PRESS

Dedicated to the actual, original George
L. K.

This is a work of fiction. Names, characters, places, and incidents are either products of the author's imagination or, if real, are used fictitiously.

Text copyright © 2013 by Liz Kessler
Illustrations copyright © 2013 by Mike Phillips
Candlewick Sparks®. Candlewick Sparks is a registered trademark of Candlewick Press, Inc.

All rights reserved. No part of this book may be reproduced, transmitted, or stored in an information retrieval system in any form or by any means, graphic, electronic, or mechanical, including photocopying, taping, and recording, without prior written permission from the publisher.

First published in Great Britain by Orion Children's Books,
a division of the Orion Publishing Group

First U.S. paperback edition 2015

Library of Congress Catalog Card Number 2013944005
ISBN 978-0-7636-6751-1 (hardcover)
ISBN 978-0-7636-8031-2 (paperback)

15 16 17 18 19 20 TLF 10 9 8 7 6 5 4 3 2 1

Printed in Dongguan, Guangdong, China

This book was typeset in Badger.
The illustrations were done in ink and watercolor.

Candlewick Press
99 Dover Street
Somerville, Massachusetts 02144

visit us at www.candlewick.com

Contents

CHAPTER
One

Poppy the Pirate Dog was bored.

She was home alone.

Again.

Over the summer, she'd read books about pirates with Tim.

She'd found buried treasure with Suzy.

She'd worn her skull-and-crossbones scarf and had pirate adventures every day.

But now Tim and Suzy had gone back to school and Mom and Dad were at work all day. And Poppy's scarf had been in the laundry for weeks.

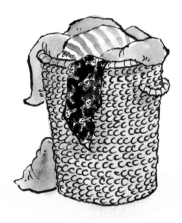

After Tim got home from school one day, he noticed Poppy lying by the door. "Would you like to hide some pirate treasure?" he asked.

Poppy wagged her tail. At last someone was going to play with her!

Poppy grabbed her favorite orange sock with the hole in it and ran over to the couch. She nudged it under a cushion.

"Good job, Poppy," said Tim. "I bet no one will ever find it there!"

Next they took Poppy's red squeaky ball and hid it deep in the bottom of Tim's closet.

Then they took Poppy's best bone and hid it behind the garage.

"That was fun, Poppy," Tim said as he patted her head. "No one will ever find our treasures! But now I've got to go to soccer. See you later!" Poppy whimpered as he walked away, leaving her all alone again.

"I think Poppy's lonely," Tim said that night at dinner.

Of course I'm lonely, Poppy
thought. *You try spending all day in an
empty house and see how you feel!*

"I think you're right," said Suzy as she tied Poppy's freshly washed scarf around her neck. "A pirate dog like Poppy needs shipmates — not an empty house!"

So they came up with a plan.
Dad made some phone calls after
dinner. Then he said, "We can go over
tomorrow morning!"

"You'll have a new shipmate soon, Poppy," Tim said.

A new shipmate, thought Poppy, one that doesn't have to go to school or to work!

Before bed, Suzy said good night to Poppy. "Just think, tomorrow you're going to have a little brother!" Suzy said.

A little brother for a shipmate, Poppy thought. *I bet he'll be just like me!*

Poppy paced the house all night, thinking about the things she would do with her new little brother.

She would teach him all about
being a pirate dog, and she could show
him how to hide his treasure.

She'd curl up with him at night, and maybe he would get his own skull-and-crossbones scarf, just like hers.

CHAPTER Three

When the family came back the next morning, Poppy charged down the stairs to meet her new brother.

"Poppy, this is George," Suzy said.
Poppy leaped up to see what she was
holding in her arms. Then she froze.
This couldn't be right.

Poppy stared at the ball of orange fluff in Suzy's arms. It had huge eyes and little whiskers around its mouth.

Suzy smiled. "He's a kitten!" she said.

The kitten reached one of its tiny paws toward Poppy. Ouch! It had claws — and they hurt!

Suzy put George on the ground.
George stared at Poppy. Poppy sniffed
George. Then Poppy turned around
and walked off to lie on her bed. This
George was not her brother — and
definitely *not* her new shipmate!

That night, no one came by to give Poppy her nighttime snuggles, so Poppy went to find them. They were all in Mom and Dad's room, sitting on the bed.

And in the middle of the bed —
right where Poppy was *never* allowed
to sit — was George! Everyone was
saying things like "Awwww, he's so
cute" and "Oooh, look at his little
paws!" *He's certainly no pirate,* Poppy
thought as she curled up on her bed
by herself.

CHAPTER
Four

On Monday morning, Suzy and Tim
went to school and Mom and Dad
went to work. Poppy lay on her bed,
more miserable than ever. It was worse
than being alone—now she would
have to spend all day with George!

She heard a splashing sound
coming from the kitchen, so she went
to investigate.

George was having a drink out of
her water bowl! Poppy growled, and
George wiped his whiskers with one of
his tiny paws and skipped away.

Poppy went back to her bed and tried to sleep, but she was too mad. Then she heard a shuffling sound. Poppy looked at the sofa. The treasure she'd hidden with Tim — her favorite orange sock — was moving!

Poppy picked up the sock in her mouth. It was heavier than she remembered. "Mmmeeeeooooowww!"

Poppy dropped the sock.
Something was inside it!

She picked up the sock again and
shook it. The tip of a tail poked out,
then two paws. One more shake, and
George plopped onto the floor!

She marched across the room with
the sock, dropped it on her bed, and
sat down on it.

From now on, she would guard
it with her life! At least George would
never find her other treasures, she
thought. They were too well hidden.

Then she heard a squeaking noise coming from Tim's bedroom. Poppy ran to the doorway and saw Tim's closet door open. Inside was George. And he was jumping up and down on Poppy's red squeaky ball!

Poppy barked loudly. George froze. He looked at Poppy with his big round eyes.

Poppy nosed George out of the
way and took her ball back to her bed.

She would watch all her treasure
like a hawk from now on.

Poppy was still guarding her treasure when she felt something pounce on her tail.

George!

That was it! Poppy had had enough.

She leaped off her bed and
growled her most fearsome, angry
pirate growl. George arched his back
and hissed like a snake.

Poppy barked and chased George
through the kitchen. Then George
leaped onto the door handle and the
door swung open.

Finally, Poppy thought as she walked back to her bed, *I've got the house to myself again.*

CHAPTER
Five

After Poppy woke up from a long nap, she noticed that it was very quiet. Too quiet. She went outside to see what George was up to now.

Poppy searched the yard. She
sniffed the bushes and the flower beds,
but no George.

Then she saw him. George had
found her last treasure — her best
bone — behind the garage, and he was
sitting on the wall, nibbling on it!

Poppy barked, and George
bounded off the wall.

Poppy chased him through the
flowers and across the grass right to
the edge of the pond.

George took a flying leap into
the air and landed on a lily pad in the
middle of the pond. Poppy skidded to
a stop.

He can stay there! Poppy thought. *That will teach him to mess with a pirate dog.*

Poppy turned to go back into the house, but then she heard George meowing.

She turned around and saw
George scrambling around, trying to
stay on the lily pad while it slipped and
slid underneath him.

She started to feel a little bit sorry for George. After all, he wasn't a tough pirate like herself. She looked at the wooden ramp that led into the pond. The only way to reach him would be to walk the plank.

"Meeooowww!" cried George loudly as he started to slide off the lily pad into the water.

Poppy tiptoed carefully onto the plank. She stretched out as far as she could.

George leaned toward Poppy, and
Poppy reached toward George.

She reached her nose a bit farther
and grabbed George.

She carefully pulled him to safety,
carried him across the plank, and set
him down on the grass.

Poppy sat down, too. She still wasn't ready to forgive George for stealing her treasure, but he did look sorry. Maybe it was time to go back inside.

Poppy picked up her bone and walked back to the house with George following along beside her.

She took the bone straight to her bed with her other treasure. "Meow!" said George as he tried to climb onto her bed. Poppy looked at him. He *was* pretty cute. But he also had very pirate-like claws and a scary hiss.

Later that day, Suzy and Tim burst through the door when they got home from school.

"George!" Suzy called.

"Poppy!" Tim shouted.

They stopped when they looked
at Poppy's bed. "Mom, look!" Suzy
called.

"Poppy likes the new kitten!"

He's not a kitten, Poppy thought, snuggling a bit closer. *He's my new shipmate!*